Snake is Going Away!

D1312845

Alison Hawes

Illustrated by Charlotte Combe

RIGBY

"I am going away," said Snake.

"Look!" said Hippo.
"Snake is going away for ever!"

Snake's House

5

"Look!" said Giraffe.
"Snake is going away for ever!"

Snake's House

"Look!" said Monkey.
"Snake is going away for ever!"

Snake's House

9

"Don't go away for ever, Snake!" said Monkey.

10

Snake's House

11

"I'm not going away for ever," said Snake.

"I'm going away on holiday!"

15